KEVIN MARSHALL

Love on the Moon

First edition

This book was professionally typeset on Reedsy.
Find out more at reedsy.com

Dedication

This book is for anyone who has ever felt bad about being different.

Contents

Foreword

Love on the Moon is a love story. It's a journey through all phases and cycles of love; The butterflies you feel when you meet someone special, the liberation you feel when you discover the importance of self-love, and the pain you feel when a loved one is ripped away from you.

The writings in this book transcend time and space. Love on the Moon is art, in its truest form. Art is energy. I invite and encourage your own interpretation of each poem. Think about the book in pieces. Think about what each word means to you. Think about it as a whole. What does this book reflect in your own lives?

I really hope you fall in love with this book, as I have.

Acknowledgement

This book was written in memory of Roethal "Elf" Pratt (1923-2021). Love you, to the Moon and back.

I

LOVE

Love On The Moon.

Damn, your eyes are taking me higher:
Up from the clouds, away from the flowers.
I'm hoping there's somewhere we can go next.
I'd be disappointed if tonight's already over.
Your teeth are like stars.
Damn, you're solar.
They're beaming so bright,
Can I hold you?

Let's rocket to the Moon.
Damn, we're soldiers.
Or we can float on these vibes,
Ditch this Rover.

I'll face my demons if I'm home alone.
I hate being home alone.
Let's go above the clouds with all our problems.
When I'm with you, I don't have to solve them.

Far from the hate, far from doom,
Damn, let's just go…
Let's make love on the Moon.

By The Ocean.

I had a dream that we were dancing by the ocean,
The moonlight illuminating our silhouettes.
Our footsteps made temporary prints in the sand,
Moments before the wetness forcefully hid our tracks.

That warm summer night,
We danced under the peacefully perfect moonlight,
Unknowingly serving as entertainment for an on-looking whale.

The giant whale traversed to the shore and swallowed us whole.
And there, in the belly of the whale, we settled.
We were in a dimension where time and space didn't matter:
Nothing mattered anymore.

We made a home in the whale,
We raised a family right there, in that very whale.

We proved that no matter where we were,
Whether dancing on the beach,
Or in the belly of a whale,
We would be together forever.

Red Euphoria/ Uh oh.

The sky is on fire!
The red and orange merged together and created a sky that reminded me of
Rainbow sherbet.
It was an unusually warm winter day, with temperatures in the mid-60s:
The perfect weather for Valentine's Day.

This Valentine's Day was liberating, euphoric even.
You'd ask me to meet you at a house in East Atlanta.

I quickly unrobed and turned on the water,
Placing a couple of fingers under the faucet
To make sure the liquid was piping hot.
Steam quickly filled the bathroom as I glanced at my phone.
Uh oh, if I don't hurry,
I'll be late.

I grabbed my custom-made jacket.
I paired it with light grey slacks and black dress shoes.
After a few splashes of cologne, I was ready to go.

By this time, the lava in the sky had subsided.
The ash-colored sky signaled the start of our evening.

I arrived at the house and eagerly opened the door,

Immediately greeted by a sea of candles.
Uh oh, here come the butterflies.

You made dinner and we painted portraits.
Towards the Sun, remember?

We painted using the colors of the sky.
Yours wasn't very good, mine probably wasn't either,
But you made me feel like Leonardo da Vinci.

In that moment we connected.
Uh oh, my guard is slowly coming down.
I feel like I'm losing control…
I love that feeling.
There's something so enjoyably inconvenient about losing yourself in love.

Fugitives.

I'm so new to this.
Let's pack our bags and run away,
Be fugitives.

While some may argue that it's immature and foolish,
We can be an example that "happily ever after" does exist.

Let's hurry before we change our minds.
All we need are the essentials,
Let's not waste more time.

Deodorant, underwear, and a fresh smile,
We don't need gasoline,
We'll use love to travel mile by mile.

Holding hands as we traverse the hills of life,
Breaking societal norms like husband and wife.
While the mild summer sun
And our adult responsibilities are beaming on our backs,
We forget all of our cares
And our problems.
We relax.

The radio's blasting
But the words don't resonate.
Too busy thinking of a world filled with more love and less hate.
How we were born pure with no hate,
But somehow managed to be contaminated,
It's hard to let resonate.

It's almost like love has become a crime.
Why can one group love freely and we have to remain so blind?
Only one form of love is justifiable…
Is that what you're telling me?
You can be manipulated if you want
But I refuse to buy what they're selling me.

You want me to be blind so badly
That I can barely see.
Visionless or not,
If that's the case,
Charge me with a felony.

I have to be true to me,
Let's break out of this worldly jail,
Get on the highway and flee.
I'm too old to feel so new to this…
But if loving you is a crime,
Let's be fugitives.

Black.

I would have to say black,
I love being black.
Black has so much meaning behind it.

While black can symbolize hurt,
Pain, and
Dark emotions,
It's such a beautiful color.

Black represents night.
It also reminds me that neither night
Nor darkness will last forever.

Black represents my ancestors,
Their heritage and history.
Black represents power.
One day, I'll build my black empire.

Black represents elegance and mystery,
It reminds me to never give everyone everything:
Keep some secrets for me.

Black also represents fear:
Fear of the unknown,

Fear of what's to come,
Fear of the future.

But
Fear can be good.
Fear is a good motivator.

II

HEARTBREAK

All These Ours.

Living for the weekend,
Rushing precious days.
Who came up with the concept of work, weekends, or time anyway?
I never thought that the last time
Would be the last time.
Here in the flesh.
Here on earth.
I couldn't say goodbye,
Which makes it worse.
I wonder if God is up above counting hours?
Making sure we realize that these moments are His,
Not ours.
He probably has each of our lives on a stopwatch.
I wonder if death came that day and just watched us.
Did death wait until after that FaceTime,
When I last saw you?
I probably need to start appreciating every moment.
No more lines,
No more Starbucks.
Too tired to wake up,
Wasting hours.
I still remember how stiff your body was
When I got the call.
I know I'll see you again one day,

Whether it be years,
Months,
Or hours.
I'll be waiting, keeping the memories close.
My memories,
Ours.

Lie To Me.

Like a bird born with the ability to fly,
The ability to love is something we should all
Have until the day we die.
The truth would have kept me in your nest,
So I asked you to lie.

Lie to me, or in the alternative,
Fly to me.
I needed one or the other,
So that you could die to me.

You did neither, instead,
You said you would die for me.
When the sight of you still gives me chills,
I need you to die for me.

Baby, you give me life, a twisted paradise.
All of this, just off one kiss, this can't be right.
Tired as hell tonight,
I couldn't sleep last night.
Why can't you sacrifice?
Nicknamed you Hell on Ice.

Yea, this is Hell all right.

Red horns and dynamite.
I told you to go to Hell last night.
I know that wasn't Christian-like.

Tell me I'm a lazy lover,
I'm ugly,
You wouldn't date me,
Tell me you love another.
I'm not the one,
Please tell me you hate me.

Tell me anything, so that I can fly.
No matter what you say,
Please just lie.

Brown Magic.

I gazed into your eyes.
Your mouth was moving and
I imagine words were coming out,
But the words fell on deaf ears.
I was hypnotized by your eyes,
Your pine-painted, oval eyes.
Brown Magic

Your eyes told a story,
A story of purpose and pain,
How you survived the most harrowing life experiences.
Your eyes revealed your inner beauty,
They showed the scars that you've never revealed.

I stared down into the brown magic,
Floating over clear mountains.
I lifted the glass and took a quick sip,
Man, that burned!

Grabbed the dove-dyed napkin
And wiped the corners of my mouth quickly,
While glancing at your chocolate skin.

The light from the candle illuminated your tone.

Your skin was so dark,
So alluring,
It was magic.
Brown Magic

The toxicity of the bourbon began to poison me,
I could barely keep from blushing.
This magic was so strong and potent.

I invited you here for a reason though,
I could not be distracted.
I had waited so long for closure,
I deserved it.

The waiter came and asked if we would like another round.
I looked down at the evaporated toxic in my glass.
I was enjoying the moment so much that
I didn't notice I had finished my drink.

We both declined,
Then continued traversing the conversation.

My wet dream abruptly came to an end
When I heard the word "friends."

It was a punch in the chest.

I quickly tried to recover —
Perhaps your statement was a result of the brown magic in your glass.
Maybe the bark-colored liquid had made
You slur something that you didn't mean.

I don't know what hurt more,

The rejection or the realization that you would never be mine.
The sorcery of your words left me bewildered.

After that, we chatted for a bit,
Talked a little about music to ease the pain of the burn.

Selling Secrets.

I'm going broke and quickly losing hope.
Empty pockets, no golden lockets,
Nothing to pawn, no money to be made,
Nothing to barter, sell or trade.

But I do have all the valuable secrets
That I've kept bottled away,
Locked tight in the confines of my brain.

Some I've kept close to my heart.
Then a voice whispered to me and said,
"You would sell them, if you were smart."

Some of them are comical,
Some of them sharp,
I'd be a millionaire if I sold everything they've done in the dark.

An auction to the highest bidder!
Not sure how much I should sell them for,
I'm only a beginner.

Just get the cash and dash.
I'll even sell my own secrets,
Her first and my last.

SELLING SECRETS.

What I did when I was twenty-something,
Secrets about where you've been
And how you're fronting.

Why would I be trustworthy?
There's no fun in that.
For a couple of bands,
I'll be the neighborhood rat.

I'm selling secrets because
I've been sold out too.
If loyalty is worth nothing,
What else should I do?

Goliath's Home.

I nervously walked through the two dove-white pillars headed towards
The giant doors of the mega-mansion.
The home was tucked away in the upscale Buckhead community of Atlanta.

The home was huge and breathtaking.
Goliath's home

I quickly pulled down my mask before entering the place of dwelling.
This "Phantom of the Opera" mask only covered half of my face.
My date and I clasped hands as a display of affection
As the other couples stared.
All of their masks looked expensive and complemented their looks.
I didn't fit in here.

In the sea of patrons floated a collection of beautiful
Gold, red, and blue dresses.
The gentlemen were dressed in traditional tuxedos, with mainly black masks.
The music was dull and classic.
The women giggled at the latest gossip in their ugly designer gowns.

The white dress shirt choked my neck
As I adjusted my midnight painted clip-on bowtie.
I knew that they could tell I wasn't used to this.

I quickly grabbed a glass of champagne.
The bubbles tickled my throat as I sipped the liquid depressant.
Smile.
Breathe.
Look entertained!
Don't walk too fast.
Not so slow.
The little voice in my head whispered.

I glanced at my watch to see the time.
It was almost midnight and I wasn't even buzzed.
I sipped the champagne again, this time the sip was longer.

Honestly, this masquerade party is a bunch of fake-ass people
Hiding behind masks.
People pretending to enjoy where they are and who they are with.

My heart dropped a little when you walked by.
You gave a quick hug,
One that wasn't too long.
A long hug would have raised eyebrows.
This one was quick enough to show polite affection,
But
Long enough to communicate without words.
The wordless hug spoke to me.

If actions speak louder than words, this was a scream.
I clasped hands with my date
And
Continued to squirm through the sea of patrons.

Throughout the night, you would walk by to see if I would look.
We would make eye contact at times but quickly break contact.

In between artificial laughs,
I would look across the room to see if I could find you.

As the night went on, I realized more and more
That
I fit right in with the patrons that I loathed so much.
I realized that I was just as fake as them.

I was here with someone else,
While wishing you were my date.
I felt more from our hug than I felt that entire evening.
I was pretending to have a good time when I wasn't.
I was pretending to be happy for you when I wasn't.

I wanted to text you, but I couldn't muster up the strength.
I adjusted my mask and gulped a fresh swallow of bitter depressant.

I adjusted my mask a little and prepared for the evening toast.
I forced a smile as we gathered around the podium.

Cheers to your engagement.

III

HATE

I Cried For You.

It was one of the hardest decisions I've ever had to make,
One that makes you toss and turn at night.
A nagging decision that wakes you up at
4 a.m. and holds you hostage.

I was broken-hearted,
Devastated even.
I loved you almost more than I loved myself.

It was one of the hardest decisions
I've ever had to make.
One that makes your brain hurt from thinking about it so much.
This was a decision that you ruminate on for hours, days, and months.

A decision that makes you analyze all the possible scenarios,
Trying your best to salvage the relationship.

I tried to find a reason to save the friendship,
Even after you humiliated me.
During our phone call,
I quietly begged for a reason to stay in the game.

It was one of the hardest decisions I've had to make,
A terrifying decision that hurts so bad you cry at night.

I cried for you,
When I decided to choose me.

I Saw The Devil In My House.

With rage in your eyes and bullets on your lips,
I saw the devil.

When you raise your hand,
You don't quit and I tried my hardest not to quit.

There was blood on my chest and love in my eyes.
At that moment, I saw the devil in my house.

The cuts on my face started to sting.
I prayed the operator would pick up on my first ring…

The Realist.

Can I be real for a minute?
This year, I've been feeling like "fuck this."
You give all you can, but you still don't win.
Fell out with a couple of people I considered close friends,
Swallowed all my feelings in some Hennessy,
And then there's therapy.

Some things shouldn't have to be explained,
Things like loyalty and honesty.
Let me pour another glass of Hennessy,
I need my fucking key.
Mail it to me.

Then I see the pictures of your new life.
You're smiling and you're happy,
But I thought you only had love for me.

They destroy all that's real and wonder why everything is fake.
Going there with me was a big mistake.

Life's so damn hard for the real ones.

Mars Is Overrated.

I wanted to confront you.
I was planning to pull you to the side
And give you a piece of my mind.

I wanted to look good doing it,
So I worked out at least three times a week.
I was on a mission
And I wouldn't stop until I achieved my goal.

I changed my diet,
I even made a conscious effort to push through leg day.
I wanted to look my best,
Not for me, but for you.

I wanted to hate you.
I needed to.

I wanted you to feel the same pain that I felt.
I wanted you to feel my embarrassment, my shame.
I wanted you to feel lonely, depressed even.
I wanted you to be alone and desperate — like me.
I needed you to feel all the emotions that I felt.
To feel the beautiful pain and the magnificent hurt,
The aching and the breaking.

While my hate was manifesting, you were still living.
Unbeknownst to you, my hate proved to poison me.
Hating you was hurting me.

War is overrated.

Diagnose me.

I want to hear you tell me why
I'll **never** be good enough.

I told you my symptoms,
Even explained where the pain was coming from
But you failed to listen.

You recommend something to mask my pain,
Not cure me.
I sat on the phone with bated breath,
Wishing you would just get it over with.

We both know what's wrong with me,
Go ahead and say it.
Diagnose me!

I know you'll never accept me.
So, just do it.
Tell me what my problem is.
Please just,
Diagnose me!

Why does it matter now anyway?
People like us can get married,

Live a "normal" life.
We don't have to worry about being stoned
Or killed for who we like.

No matter how much I accomplish,
No matter how smart I am,
I will never be good enough and we both know why.
Get it over with, I can take it.
I'm what?
Diagnose me!

Tell me what's wrong with me.
Tell me that I can be healed through lying and pretending.
Fuck it,
Go ahead,
Diagnose me!

IV

APATHY

Engagement.

Ain't getting as much love with the name change.
We're all too consumed with likes and engagement.
Everyone's selling their soul for a repost.
Less concerned with where they live or their car getting repossessed.

Who are you?
Without all the filters and the follows.
Who am I, outside of the quotes and the lonely smile?

Show more skin,
Be funny for engagement.
Dumb yourself down,
All for engagement.

Nobody wants to think,
It's all about engagement.

Less merchandise, no more books.
My family wants grandkids,
A girlfriend,
An engagement.

What do I want?
It seems like I'm doing this for everybody else.

Starting to care more about posting pictures,
Rather than the big picture.

Give away my body and have some kids,
A family.
Not in the name of love,
Only to please my family.

Sometimes, I wish life was easier.
A wife,
Some kids,
A house in the suburbs with little engagement,
What the "normal" people have.

The Problem With Saturn.

A life full of fancy things
With a crew full of stars and
A wrist full of rings.

You've got a beautiful hue
And a boatload of bling,
There's no need to be smart,
No one cares what you think.

One of the oldest around
Yet still waiting to bloom.
Who cares about substance?
You're the brightest in the room.

Among a million planets
Yet still lonely in space,
So what that you're toxic inside,
You have a beautiful face.

I'm Sorry.

I'm sorry,
But I can't apologize.

I still remember all the anger,
The rage in your eyes
With venom on your lips,
And hate in that glass of red wine.

They all called asking me to apologize.
I know they could hear the ego in my voice,
I had already made up my mind.

She kept screaming, "She just died!"
We forget that we are on the same side.

Look, if it makes things better,
I'm sorry.
But
I can't apologize for finally setting boundaries.

I'm Terrified of People.

Sometimes, I wake up feeling like a dartboard
With friends and enemies alike
Vying for a chance to strike another dart
Smack dab in the center of my back.

Never thought much about what my greatest fear was.
At one point,
I thought it was dying like Uncle Brian
Or falling to my untimely demise

Truth is, I'm terrified of people.
The last person I trusted
Made my heart stop in the middle of a strip club.

Took everything in me not to react to that.
I just let it pass,
Act like I didn't hear it.
Be the bigger person,
Whatever that means.

How much more can I take?
The monsters under my bed don't scare me.
It's the people —
Their lies, you know?

How humans shift so quickly,
They move on to the next best thing.
Something newer, fresher, younger,
How **things** are valued more than **people...**
That scares me!

I've met quite a few clowns,
They don't scare me much.
I've even come face to face with snakes that don't hiss.

Never thought much about what my greatest fear is.
I think my greatest fear is people.

Jaded.

A Band-Aid and a blank page
A cup of hurt and a dash of rage

The darkroom had to fade to black…
I even tried finding myself on a dating app.

Drowning in sorrow,
Yet still searching for that one marine.
That's what happens when
You let strangers play with your self-esteem.

The tides are changing
And
With every wave that washes,
I feel less enthused with love,
But maybe it's just my options.

It all comes down to my emotions
(Or lack thereof).
And yea, I'm a nice guy,
But maybe I don't deserve love.

If I ever got it again, I might not feel it.
Last time it left me crippled:

I ran into love, but I couldn't walk out with it.

Baby, my heart's got thorns.
If you try to touch it, you might get pricked.
Who's going to love me when I'm old?
Love me when I'm sick?

Slow burn, I just faded.
I wrote back on the app and said I've seen it before,
You're not crazy…
You're just jaded.

V

HOPE

Mr. Nice Scars.

I'd love to know why God allowed us to have scars.
God could have easily chosen to make the skin heal perfectly,
Back to its original form before the wound

But
God chose to have the skin grow back differently.
Almost to signify that something awesome happened in that very location.
Why do you think that God made that decision?

Perhaps a scar is to serve as a reminder of the event that transpired.
A reminder of how we healed…
And
Grew from that event.

Perhaps scars were meant to be a conversation starter
So that others can connect with
Art used to describe pain.

Our scars remind us that the past was real.
Something that hurt, throbbed and bled is
Now something that has healed and can cause no more pain.

Sometimes I forget about the scars,
From wounds I thought would kill me.

And
Now I think I like them.

Black Atlantis.

I washed up naked on the shore of a deserted island.
I opened my eyes to the blurry brightness of the sun,
My bare body burning on the beautiful black sand.

I vaguely remembered who I was
But I had no idea how I ended up on this island.
For two days straight, I cried.
No one is coming to save you.

I begged God to send help
But
The only answer I heard was, "Get up!"
No one is coming to save you.

I pulled myself up.
I ate berries and fruit until I learned to tie tree switches together to create
A fishing-net.

I used sticks to create a fire.
I used rocks to make weapons.
I used the weapons to kill small animals for food.
Remember,
No one is coming to save you.

As soon as I accepted the fact that I would remain on the island forever,
I saw a boat approaching.
The captain of the boat appeared to be some form of an angel.
I ran as fast as I could to the boat,
Waving my hands frantically to make sure the guests on board saw me.

Just as I reached the boat,
The annoying sound of my alarm shocked me out of my sleep.
My black sheets reminded me of the ebony sand on Black Atlantis.
No one is coming to save you.

But, Where's Black Jesus.

Kept seeing pictures of a White Jesus,
Even on Black Folks with Jesus pieces.
What's the reason?
Where's Black Jesus?

Black Jesus,
They don't read, so they'll never believe me.
It's right in the text,
But they must be hard of seeing.
This is treason!

You can show a person something,
But they have to want to see it.
You can give a person a new identity,
But they have to want to be it.

They say perspective depends on where you're seated.
Some people want to believe, they just need a reason.

Black Jesus?

All this black culture,
But they act like they don't see us.
One minute they kill us,

The next they want to be us.

My Jesus, what's the reason?
They came to Africa to get us.
Why didn't they just leave us?

No, Jesus,
He had his hands up.
Lord, why didn't they see them?

Forget that, a new CD from Yeezus.
Social media, more loans... all demons.
Where's Moses?
Where's Peter?
Where's Zeus,
White Caesar?

Only Goliath,
Only Neimen's,
All their gods are dressed in Gucci sneakers.

Maybe the trick is acting like things don't exist,
Even when all of the evidence confirms

When will Black Jesus have His turn?

Angel Food.

A tilted Halo and a golden street
With white attire and winter wings.
Flying high or running through the streets,
They have to get hungry,
But what do angels eat?

I bet that God serves them Soul Food.
Black-eyed dreams and curried hope,
Fried favor, filling faith,
I'm sure we'll all be well fed.
But I'm here on Earth eating pre-marital pudding and porn-bread.

I've tried for so long to change my appetite,
Long summer days, can't sleep at night.

I classify myself as a Christian human:
I don't see a label.
I spread God's word and,
I hope I have a seat at His table.

I convince myself that this is who I am,
I am not lost.
But being gay and black is sometimes like hot sauce.

To make a plate, I would do anything.
To get there, I've done everything.
But I drink all the time,
Didn't Jesus turn water into wine?

I've always felt like I could walk in my truth and still save souls too
But maybe I should submit to worldly standards.
Hide behind closed doors,
Like the other "so-called" Christians do.

Even in the Bible, sinners like prostitutes were used.
I just pray I don't get trashed like crumbs
When I've been working so hard to enjoy Angel Food.

I Met A Man.

The blistering cold of the Michigan Winter
Pierced my face as I exited the restaurant.
I had just finished a delicious brunch
And
Full from the meal,
Felt a spell of exhaustion possess me.

I buttoned up my blue pea-coat and
Traversed in the direction of my car.
That's when I met a man.

Unbeknownst to me,
The man had been watching me.
I'm not sure for how long or for what purpose
But he spoke to me when we made eye contact.

He was an older gentleman
With sandpaper skin
"Why aren't you smiling?" the man asked.
With a bright warm smile
That was enough to turn the cloudy sky into a sherbet oasis.

I shrugged, not sure how to respond.
"I don't know," I mumbled.

"You don't have a reason to frown.
You're alive and breathing and you have so much to be thankful for."

This man didn't treat me like any other stranger walking down the street.
His spirit was grateful and youthful,
Although you could tell that life had brought ups and downs.

Even though he had experienced times of lack,
He chose to only speak of the gold.
Though he was broken,
He chose to let his words heal.

Since that moment in 2010,
I remember daily that there is always something to smile about.
The man that I met, a "stranger,"
Taught me things that I will never forget.

He taught me to smile for every moment,
To laugh at every memory,
And
To live unapologetically.

Since that day,
I learned to take all the failures,
Disappointments,
Trials and tribulations,
And turn them all into gold.

It was the best decision of my life.
It made me the richest man in the world.

That day, I became a man.

Afterword

Love on the Moon is my story of hope. The book is a reminder that there is always hope, even during cycles of hate. We all have the opportunity to take our pain and create something beautiful, something positive, and something impactful. Everything negative, toxic, and hurtful should birth hope and a drive towards improvement.

Writing this book allowed me to take themes, conversations, and experiences, and use them to tell a story. A story that ends just like it began – with hope. Whether that is hope for love, hope for reunions on Earth and in Heaven, or hope for new beginnings.

I really hope you've fallen in love with this book, as I have.

About the Author

Kevin L. Marshall was born in Charlotte, North Carolina on August 11, 1987. He attended Elizabeth City State University, where he earned his Bachelor of Arts in Political Science. Kevin is a proud member of the Elizabeth City State University 40 Under 40 Society. In 2012, he graduated from Atlanta's John Marshall Law School.

Kevin is currently a practicing attorney in Atlanta, Georgia. He has argued at the Supreme Court of Georgia and was recognized in 2018 by the National Trial Lawyers Association as Top 40 Under 40 for civil litigation. In 2021, Kevin was recognized by The National Black Lawyers as Top 40 Under 40 for the State of Georgia. Kevin's life mission is to let everyone know, no matter who they are or where they come from, that God loves them (and he does too).

You can connect with me on:
🌐 https://kevinhashope.com

Also by Kevin Marshall

Hella Hopeful: 31 Daily Affirmations to Find Hope
Affirmations are assertions, words, or statements, which should be read and digested to shift one's mindset and thinking. This book is a thirty-one-day guide to finding hope in all aspects of your life. Each affirmation in this book contains practical assurances that will promote a life of positive thinking, peace, and abundance.

Made in the USA
Columbia, SC
11 July 2021